# THE
# AFRICAN
# BOY

# THE AFRICAN BOY

BILL WILLIAMSON

| Library of Congress Control Number: | | 2017916166 |
|---|---|---|
| ISBN: | Hardcover | 978-1-5434-8771-8 |
| | Softcover | 978-1-5434-8770-1 |
| | eBook | 978-1-5434-8769-5 |

Print information available on the last page.

Rev. date: 10/26/2017

**To order additional copies of this book, contact:**
Xlibris
800-056-3182
www.Xlibrispublishing.co.uk
Orders@Xlibrispublishing.co.uk
768596

# CONTENTS

There is a recently placed, pink granite memorial plaque in the graveyard of St Martin's church on the Isles of Scilly twenty-five miles off the coast of Cornwall in south-west England. It recalls the wreck of the brig *The Hope* in 1830 with the loss of four lives, including that of an African boy. The plaque records no name for him. We shall call him Kwame. Nor is his age mentioned. We shall say he was fourteen years old. The islanders who buried him would have learned from those who survived the wreck, that the boy came from the Gold Coast – or from what the sailors likely called 'the Guinea Coast' – and that the boat he came in had sailed from the port of Elmina and was on its way to London from where the African boy would travel further to Holland. That is all we know. There is much more to know that can now only be imagined. This is a story about him and is dedicated to his memory.

It is dedicated, too, to my grandchildren – to Ella in particular, who first drew our attention to the plaque – for Scilly remains for them all a very special place.

Proceeds from the sale of this book will be given to the Royal National Lifeboat Institution (RNLI) on the Isles of Scilly.

# CHAPTER ONE

# ON THE GOLD COAST

November 1829. It was the end of the rainy season. On the beach at Elmina, Kwame sat on the bow of his uncle's colourfully painted sea canoe, one of many that he owned, for he was a rich man. In the evening light, beyond the now quiet but incessant waves that rolled up the beach, the sea stretched like a golden, silken veil to a great orange and red sun sinking slowly below the horizon.

Its low rays cast the many anchored ships that lay in the bay into dark silhouettes. Their masts looked like the bare trees of a forest and as the evening light faded, Kwame could see the pale glow of oil lamps escaping the portholes of the white men's ships. Their voices – some shouting, some singing – cut through the sounds of people on the beach and the cluttered township beside the fort of

Elmina that had dominated this coastline since as far back as anyone could remember.

Beyond the gentle slushing sounds of the sea, Kwame could hear the familiar shrieks of squawking parrots in the dense, impenetrable and humid forest beyond the town.

He looked at the anchored vessels and remembered his uncle telling him that a long time ago, when white men first visited this shore, the people of Elmina called them *Murdele*, people of the sea, for they had no idea where they came from. Some of the older people called them *Vumbi*, their term for the ghosts of the dead. The thought amused him. He and his people knew now only too well where the white men came from and what they were like. They weren't ghosts but they behaved often like devils.

This thought passed and Kwame became aware of the smells so familiar to him that he had hardly noticed them until now during the hours before he departed for Holland. He could smell the sea and the ingrained aroma of fish from the boats mingling with the wood smoke that drifted from the town from hundreds of fires of families preparing their evening food. The light of the fading sun gave the white walled fort an orange glow that sharpened its outline and prominence over the cluttered, dark squalor of the congested streets beneath and beyond it.

From the edge of the beach towards the town, Kwame could hear the shouts and laughter coming from the wooden hovels where bearded white sailors and merchants met to drink the palm wine the town's winemakers sold to them. Sometimes, the white men got local people to drum and dance for them and they would try and join in or sing their own songs to the rhythms of the drums. Many of them ended up fighting drunk, brawling among themselves to see who could secure the company of the town's prettiest women.

Kwame had watched them on many evenings in the past and wondered how white men could behave so badly. During the day, such men worked hard loading goods onto boats. At night, on shore, they turned into devils who were best avoided. Kwame had heard of white men who had become so drunk and ill and so overcome with the heat they were not used to, that they died and had to be buried on uncultivated land near the fort.

They were not all like that. There were some, especially those who were neatly dressed and who worked in the fort and who did business with Kwame's uncle and other merchants, who never went to the beachside drinking shacks. Some, like the Dutch army officer who had agreed to take him to Holland on the English ship, *The Hope*, had a lady who was, thought Kwame, probably one of his wives. He was never drunk. He was always polite and his wife – his lady – who had accompanied him on this trip was very friendly. She had been helping Kwame to improve the Dutch language he already knew in preparation for his new life and was very keen to learn as much as possible about his family and his friends and about people in the town. He had noticed that some of the ordinary sailors looked at her with unkind grins on their pale faces and among themselves made what Kwame understood as rude remarks about her.

He'd also noted that she looked at them as if they were dirty and diseased and possessed by evil spirits. She made no attempt to acknowledge them or speak to them. She showed nothing but contempt for them and Kwame thought the men knew it. Yet with the colourfully dressed women in their *Kente* cloth garments and big headscarves who sold vegetables, fruits and fish in the shade of the palm trees that lined the beach at Elmina, the lady seemed relaxed and friendly. With the help of one of the translators from Elmina fort, she always spoke to the local woman and obviously shared funny stories with them. They clearly enjoyed each other's company.

He was not surprised at that. He liked talking to the women in the market and to the old men who sat in groups under the palm trees. He liked to visit the weavers, all of them men, who made the *Kente* cloth in their homes and who told him what the differently named colours and patterns meant. Yellow and gold colours were for royalty. Red was the colour for warriors.

They told him and his friends stories from the past. He loved to hear the tales they told about *Anansi*, the spider who could change form to become a man and who always played tricks on people. They said it was *Anansi* who spoke to the Gods to learn the stories that he told and which older people now passed on to their children. Kwame wondered if the white men had good stories to tell their children because he could not imagine living a life when people didn't sit together and tell stories.

Sometimes, the things they told him were terrifying. These old men, proud Fante tribesmen, had been warriors and had fought in wars with the Ashanti who lived in the hinterland behind the coast and deep in the forest. They had fought with white men. At other times, when they were not fighting they did business with Ashanti traders and white men earning guns and gunpowder in exchange for captured slaves. No one knew where the slaves were taken to when they were led in chains to the boats that took them out to the white men's ships anchored in the harbour.

His parents, both of whom were dead, had told Kwame that their parents, his grandparents, had been taken by Ashanti warriors and sold to Muslim traders from the desert lands in the north just as Fante traders sold captured Ashantis to the white men as slaves. These were kept in chains in the fort at Elmina and then taken away in boats, never to be seen again.

When their own parents disappeared, their uncles and his wives looked after Kwame's parents. When they were grown up, Kwame's father became a trader and a warrior. He lost his life in a battle with Ashanti raiders during one of the many clashes that took place between the coastal people and warrior raiding parties from the north. His mother died of a disease that the medicine man could not cure. Like his parents before him, his uncle and his wives looked after Kwame.

He grew up knowing that there were many from his people – the Fante – who had been taken as slaves either by Ashanti traders or white men. Those enslaved by Ashanti kings were particularly unlucky. When a king died, some of his slaves were killed so that they could accompany the dead king into the after life.

Kwame was glad he was not a slave. He felt safe in his belief that what the older people sometimes called the *Maafa*, their word for the slave trade, which in his language meant 'the great disaster', was over. Seven years before he was born, the white men from England said they would not deal in slaves any longer and the white man's boats from what they called their navy, made sure that no slave ships would ever again be allowed to sail from his land.

Kwame had never seen a slave ship. But there were slaves in Elmina who worked for the people in the fort. His uncle and his rich friends kept slaves to help grow vegetables, to build the houses of the compounds where they lived and to look after their animals and boats.

He understood that some people were slaves and had no choice in the matter. There had always been slaves in the world. What he did not understand were the white men. They were powerful. He would soon learn more about them. But sometimes their power was not enough. Just a few years ago, the Ashanti slaughtered a lot of them, including the British Governor, in a battle that the white men had fought alongside Fante warriors. How could such strong men with their guns be defeated? On the other hand, he thought, they fought back and at the battle of Bodewah, the Fante and the British together defeated an Ashanti army. Some of his friends' cousins had been killed in that battle.

Kwame was a thoughtful boy. The Dutch army officer who would take him to Holland – Major van Breggenpauwer – had told him about the wars that had taken place in his country against the French and against a man called Napoleon, the French leader. The British had defeated Napoleon both in great sea battles and on land, but despite being victors, they had spent a lot of money on war and many people living in that country were still very poor.

They had to work in factories and in coalmines; they even put their children to work in great cotton mills among dangerous, dirty machines. They lived in crowded conditions in terrible houses and their food was poor. Their big cities were dangerous places with many thieves and vagabonds. Kwame wondered what kind of place he was going to. He wasn't sure what a city or a factory was. Would there be more wars? Would he be safe?

As he sat thinking about these things, a group of his friends climbed onto the boat and sat beside him. They were always together. They swam in the sea. They went into the forest to hunt for food. They climbed trees and made swings from trailing vines. They were always on guard against danger, though, especially from snakes that would sometimes be curled up on the branches of trees. They knew that if they kept close to the paths through the forest they would be safe.

The boys had come to say goodbye because they knew Kwame would sail away from them the next morning and they did not know whether they would ever see him again. They did not know what to say. One of the friends, Amo, who was always teasing the others, said: 'You'll not be able to play *Oware* in Holland. The Dutch will be too stupid to play it!' Kwasi, who had loved their *Antonkyire* game when they were younger because he was a fast runner and always reached the knotted cloth with which the winner was allowed to beat the others, said that he'd miss him. He brought Kwame a present to take with him to Holland: a little woven bag of *Kente* cloth with palm seeds so he could play *Oware*.

Kwame felt touched by his pals' friendship; he was sad to be leaving them but also strengthened in his belief that he was no longer a child and that he must look forward to a new life as a man. He was determined to face up to that. He felt deeply that his ancestors were proud of him and would protect him. His destiny was to learn about Holland and the white man's world and return to his home and help his uncle and his family. In a way, though sad to be leaving them, he felt sorry for his friends. Their lives would be as they always have been. His would be different. He would return a 'big man' in the settlement.

Darkness sets in quickly in the tropics so the boys did not stay long by the beach. They all walked back towards their homes sad that they would not see Kwame for a long time. It was Ebo, the joker among them, who lifted their spirits momentarily so they each left one another with a smile on their faces. 'If they are nasty to you in Holland, just tell them you're a witch doctor and that you'll curse them and plague them with evil spirits! That'll frighten the arses off them!' Kofi, the serious one among them said darkly: 'You shouldn't joke about such things. Bad things might happen if you do.' But the boys just laughed as they waved goodbye to Kwame.

Kwame walked back to his compound slowly. As he left the beach, he looked up to admire the row of merchants' houses he passed on the way. His uncle had always told him he would one day be like Johan Neizer, the mixed race son of a Dutch trader and a Fante woman. He made his wealth trading with the Dutch. He had travelled a few times to Holland; he knew their language and their customs and how to trade with them. Kwame looked up to Neizer's house and imagined himself living in one just like it with a beautiful wife, servants and lots of people seeking his help and advice. He'd be known as a Big Man.

## Chapter Two

# The Journey Begins

Kwame slept restlessly that night. He was excited and worried. He felt as if he was about to do great things but anxious that he might fail. He was a confident boy and well known in the settlement with many friends. He feared he might be lonely in Holland. He hoped that his prayers to the sea spirits would ensure a safe journey but he knew, too, that the sea could be cruel and angry and that many sailors lost their lives at sea.

The captain of the ship, an Englishman, Mr Alfred Noble, seemed a kind man. He had told Kwame that on board ship he had to do as he was told. He would be a paying passenger but there were times when everyone had to help out with the work needed on board. 'On this vessel' said Captain Noble 'it's all hands to the mast'. And then he added with a stern look in his eye 'And my word is law!'

Kwame had tried on what to him were the strange clothes the Dutch officer had given him to wear on the journey, but they felt uncomfortable and coarse against his skin and he thought that the leather shoes they had given him were stiff and made it difficult to walk. Mainly, he thought that he looked stupid in these clothes and felt determined that he would wear his *Kente* cloth that his aunt had had specially made for him.

Since living near the fort, Kwame had picked up some words – quite a lot actually – of both Dutch and English from listening to sailors and fort officials and from tuning in to conversations between his uncle and Dutch traders as they talked business with the help of a Fante translator. Kwame used to pester the translators to teach him some of the white man's language and he was a fast learner.

The translators were good teachers. Like many Fante, the all knew two or three and sometimes more of the local tribal languages. They had learned the white men's languages from being with their parents who were also translators. They'd talked a lot with merchants, seamen and sailors and with the administrators in the fort. Some of them had talked a lot to some of the missionaries from Europe who in the past had tried to set up schools to teach them about their God. Some had been to such schools. There was always a lot of work for them to do and they were well paid for it. Kwame often thought that he'd like to become a translator one day.

His aunt, the one he liked best, who had looked after him after he lost his parents, woke him early and gave him food, his favourite *fufu*. She helped him dress in his Dutch clothes and gave him some fruit and some plantains for the start of the journey. She told him that the ship's cook would know how to cook the plantains.

Most important of all, she told him to look after the armband that she had given him when he was a child. It was made from brass wire twisted into patterns. This was sacred. It was his most important possession. He should pray with it. It reminded him that his ancestors were still with him and that they could keep bad spirits away from him. She told him: 'Keep it safe. Never let it out of your sight. It will protect you'.

His uncle spoke to him before he left the compound. 'Remember' he said 'you are a Fante. You must be brave and do your duty. You must say your prayers and be strong. Remember who you are. The spirits of your parents and their parents will look after you. Remember them. You will join them one day if you stay on the straight path. Come back to us. Speak their words. Learn about the white men. Do not do anything that will bring evil spirits to this home!' On that note, showing neither joy nor sadness, his uncle turned and walked back to his hut.

On the beach they met the Dutch officer and his lady, whose bags were being loaded into the canoe. The lady greeted Kwame with a smile. The Dutch officer just looked at him and said nothing. The English sailors were busy loading the canoes that supplied the ship. They were dressed in their strange clothes with broad brimmed hats. One or two of them smoked pipes. As they worked, they talked to one another and from time to time looked at Kwame and the lady and the Dutchmen in a way that Kwame thought was angry and suspicious.

He overhead one of the sailor says: 'Bloody woman! We don't want the likes of her on board!' Another said: 'Too true. Women bring bad luck on boats.' Kwame was surprised to hear this because he liked the Dutch lady.

But worse followed. The same sailor gave Kwame a withering look and then turned to his friend and said: 'We could do without that black devil as well.'

'Get in the boat, you!' yelled the sailor and gestured with his hand to make his order clear. Kwame did so and some of the men laughed at him, but not in a kindly way, because he had not rolled up his trousers or taken his shoes off to keep himself dry as he walked in the sea to the boat.

This made Kwame uneasy but matters got worse when another crew member, a man called Bidrock, pointed to Kwame's bag of food that his aunt had given him, and said: 'Wotcha got there?' Kwame did not understand exactly what the man said but did know what he meant. Not knowing what to say, Kwame opened the cloth to reveal some plantains. To the sailor, these were just like bananas and to men like him, bananas were bad news on boats. It was a fruit that rotted and became smelly quickly. Sailors believed bananas on boats attracted rats and that cargoes of bananas sometimes became a home for poisonous spiders. Without another word, Bidrock grabbed the plantains and threw them overboard. 'Yer not 'avin them on this boat, me lad' he said. Neither the Dutch officer nor the lady said anything or did anything. They just looked on. The lady was alarmed at what she saw but obviously thought it best to say nothing.

It did not take long to be rowed away from the beach to the boat that would take them to London in England where they would join a Dutch vessel to Holland. It was a 121 ton sailing brig that had been loaded with a cargo of gold dust, elephant tusks and casks of palm oil. Kwame had watched the loading throughout the previous week. When they reached the anchored brig they had to climb up a rope ladder that hung down from the gunwale of the vessel. The Dutch lady found that difficult and Kwame heard some of the crew grumbling about the fact that they had to help her up the ladder.

When the boat party got on board, they were all shocked to see that another seaman was tied by his wrists and lay on his belly across a large wooden barrel. His shirt had been pulled from his back and the first mate of the ship, with his sleeves rolled up, brought his long leather whip high above his head and lashed the sailor across his back. It was a back that showed the scars of previous, older lashings. Kwame was terrified.

What had that man done? Before he could think of an answer the whip cracked again leaving a large, red, bleeding mark on the man who yelled out in pain. They all stood in silence. Captain Noble looked down from poop deck and gestured with his hand that there should be one more lash and the mate duly gave it.

When it was over, the semi-conscious man was doused with sea water and dragged off to the foc'sle, the crew's quarters behind and under the bow of the ship and thrown into his hammock. The newly arrived passengers looked at one another, alarmed and curious and then looked up to Captain Noble in the hope of an explanation. The rest of the crew stood in silence with their heads bowed as if they daren't speak. The captain said: 'This man came from shore drunk. You were all told that there was to be no drink before we set sail. A drunken sailor is no use to man nor beast. He has been punished. You all know the rules. Now get to work!' He turned on his heels, his hand on the stock of his gun and walked determinedly to his cabin. As he did so, he turned to the first mate and said: 'We sail in an hour!'

The first mate, a man by the name of Boydell, led the Dutchman and his lady to their cabin and on returning to the deck indicated with a gesture that Kwame should follow him to the foc'sle to where he would sleep in the crew's quarters. He sensed this was a man who, like the captain, was at all times to be obeyed.

He followed the mate down a ladder into a dark, low-ceilinged space with hammocks strung from above that hovered above tables and benches where the crew took their food. The mate pushed Kwame towards the narrowest part of the foc'sle where his hammock was and to where there was a roughly made cupboard in which he could put his things. On the tables there were candles and metal plates.

As he left Kwame, the mate turned to him and said; 'They'll show you the ropes' and left. But for one sailor – a young man called Hicks – who sat with his pipe watching, there was only one other in the cramped room. That was the curled body of the whipped sailor – Croft – who lay groaning in pain in his hammock at the far side of the foc'sle away from Kwame.

Kwame felt as if he'd been put in a box and that someone had closed the lid. As his eyes adjusted to the darkness, he noticed more. There were bedrolls in each hammock. There were hooks on the ship's timbers where sailors hung their coats. What he noticed most of all was that no one was helping the injured sailor. He wondered if he should but did not know what he could do to help. The man needed water, he thought. On the floor, near his berth he noticed a large wooden bucket with a rope handle. He wondered if this was the place from which to get the sailor a drink.

As if reading Kwame's mind, the pipe-smoking sailor, Hicks said: 'That's for pissin' in! And it's your job to empty and wash it every morning!' 'The Heads is upstairs'. 'Heads' wondered Kwame. What are the 'Heads? He knew what the English word meant: heads were heads and everyone had one with eyes and noses and ears and mouths. What did the man mean when he said they were upstairs? Kwame tried to ask him but didn't yet know enough English to say it properly so he merely looked as if he was asking a question and repeated the word 'Heads?' 'They're for shittin' in' said the sailor 'and be sure you keep them clean' and to reinforce the point so that Kwame understood him, he pointed to his own bum and made farting noises and laughed till his body shook as he explained this.

With a broad grin on his bearded face he then said: ' Now let's see yer 'op in to yer hammock'. Again, Kwame was not exactly sure what the man had said but sensed enough that he was being asked to get into his bed. Try as he could, he failed each time. If he put his leg in first, the hammock just swung away from his body. If he tried to pull himself in with his hands and arms, it just turned upside down.

The sailor stood and said: 'Look here. This is how it's done. He stood up. He climbed onto the table below the hammock and turned so that he could sit on the hammock and then leant backwards to lie flat in it. 'Ye see' he said, 'Get yer arse in first' and lay there laughing, his brown-stained teeth clearly visible. 'What kind of people are these?' wondered Kwame.

A bell rang and the sailor practically hopped out of the hammock and left the foc'sle to go on deck. Kwame tried to get into the hammock as the sailor had and did so at the first attempt. As he lay there, the hammock gently swaying with the movement of the ship, he thought to himself that this was a comfortable bed. He lay there for a few moments listening to the sounds of the boat: the creaking timbers, the slip-slap of the sea against the hull, the sharp shouts from above as orders were given and men replied with 'Aye Aye'. He could hear the sounds of men walking and sometimes running on the deck above. Above all, he could hear the sailor groaning and sobbing, lost in a world of pain without either help or hope.

The air in the foc'sle was muggy and damp. The place stank of stale smoke, old food and the sweat soaked into dirty clothes. Kwame decided he needed fresh air and left to climb the ladder to the deck.

As always, it was a warm breeze that greeted him rich in the smell of the sea. He could hear gulls above the high masts of the ship and sailors were hauling on ropes to hoist her sails. He walked over to where the Dutchman and his lady were standing observing all the work being done. As the sails caught the wind, the boat seemed to lurch forward. The crew hauling the anchor from the sea were chanting some kind of song that Kwame thought helped them with their work. The captain and the mate shouted orders from the poop deck and the ship almost leapt to life as it left its anchorage and its bow swung around to the open sea.

Kwame had anticipated this moment for a long time. He had hoped to feel happy about starting this journey, this adventure. But he didn't feel happy. He felt sad about leaving his home and he worried about these white people. He could not properly understand all they said. He thought they were cruel and ugly and not very clean. Some of them clearly did not obey their leaders and masters. He had no idea what he would eat and he was feeling hungry. At home, he went to his toilet in the forest. Where would he do it on board ship? At home, his uncle's slaves emptied the night buckets. Would they trap him into slavery? No, he thought, the Dutch officer had given his word to his uncle. He would look after me and, he thought, like Johan Neizer, I'll be safe in Holland.

His eyes and his mind were kept busy watching all the movement and activity on deck and he was curious to see how these ships were made to sail. When he looked back, he noticed that land seemed far off. From the sea, he could still see the outlines of the Elmina fort and the houses of the settlement. He could also see from on board something he had never seen before: the hills behind the dense forest and its great expanse stretching further than the eye could see far from the coast into Ashanti land. He had never imagined the world was as big as this. He said a silent prayer to his ancestors to look after him and to the sea spirit to keep the boat safe.

# CHAPTER THREE

# AT SEA

It did not take long for the ship to be so far from shore that land just appeared as a thin strip of greyish blue, marking out a line between the sea and the sky. Looking ahead into the open sea, Kwame could only see a vast, empty expanse of water no longer the light green colour of the water nearer home but dark blue, almost black in colour.

The ship was full of sounds: of the gusting of wind against the sails, of creaking timbers and of the sea slapping against the bows. Cutting through were the sounds of voices: of shouted orders from the captain or the mate and of men answering back. There was plenty of movement on board, of men pulling on ropes or swabbing the deck with mops or scurrying down below carrying buckets of water for the cook in the ship's galley. And there was lots of talking and grumbling and sometimes singing as the sailors went about their work. Then there were the bells, sounded when it was time for some men to take their rest or to eat their food or to change watch. Kwame had never had any reason to think about what time of day it was but on board he quickly learned that every four hours, even through the night, the ship's bell signalled the time for sailors to either to start their work or take their rest.

The Dutch officer's wife told Kwame that sailors often sang when they had to work together because the songs, which the English called 'sea shanties', helped them to get through their tasks. She liked to hear them sing and said it was at least better than hearing them curse and swear at one another.

Kwame was keen to learn the ways of the ship and when he could, he helped the men to do their work. He carried fresh water to the cook. He helped at the pumps that had to be worked regularly to clear the water from the bilges of the ship. It was hard work but he enjoyed it, working in unison with the sailors who sometimes sang as they worked and the songs helped give a rhythm to their work that made it easier and took the tedium of it away. He swabbed and dried the deck. He liked to oil the masts and other woodwork to protect the wood from the effects of salt water and the drying wind. He enjoyed listening to the sailors talking to one another and in this way picked up a good understanding of their English. He also got to know the sailors and to know which ones he had to be careful with.

He learned about one of them – Bidrock – the one who had thrown his plantains overboard, the hard way. This man was grumpy and was always complaining about one thing or another. Kwame didn't like him and when he explained this to Hicks, the sailor he had met in the foc'sle on his first day on board, he was warned to be careful of Bidrock whose temper was terrible.

Kwame liked Hicks. He was younger than the other sailors and he was interested to talk to Kwame. Kwame was interested in him, too, because he played the fiddle. He was the ship's 'shanty man' who on a calm evening at sea after all the work was done would often play his fiddle to entertain the others. He also prompted the others to sing when they were working.

When Hicks played the fiddle, Kwame often added an accompaniment of drumming – banging on an upturned bucket with a marling pin – or clapping his hands while he danced to the tune. This entertained everyone except Bidrock. There was not a trace of fun in the man. He never laughed, he never smiled; the words that passed his lips were either grumbles or curses and he made it clear to Kwame that he must keep away from him. He wanted nothing to do with 'black devils'.

One evening after an hour or so of Hick's fiddle playing, Bidrock turned away from those on deck to go down below. As he did so, Kwame pretended to follow him and to walk like him. Like many sailors used to life on deck, Bidrock walked with a swaying movement with his legs wide apart. His legs were in any case bowed, probably on account of childhood rickets which made his walk look even funnier, at least to Kwame.

Kwame liked teasing people and followed Bidrock imitating his walk and as he did so the others laughed. Just as they did so Bidrock turned around and, realising what they were laughing at, became instantly angry and shouted at Kwame and swung his arm to clip the boy around the ears. Luckily, Kwame was too quick for him and ducked out of the way and fortunately, too, did not understand the stream of abuse that came from Bidrock's lips as he yelled at him.

The first mate, Boydell, who had been standing on the poop deck on look out, shouted at the group on deck. 'Stop that commotion! Get to your hammocks! This is an orderly ship.' Boydell was not a man to be ignored. He was a man able to show his authority. He was strong and fearless and insisted on good discipline. He looked sternly at Bidrock and pointed at him to go in the direction of the foc'sle stairs with no further grumbling. As he did so, Bidrock cast a quick and angry glance at Kwame as if to say, 'You'll suffer for this!'

Kwame was shocked and puzzled but Hicks patted him on the back and said; 'Never mind him; he'll not harm you. I'll see to that. But watch out for 'im; he can be nasty'.

The other sailors on deck – Smith, Jackson the cook and Croft, the man who had been whipped at the start of the voyage and, of course, Hicks – moved off to do their remaining work for the evening, leaving Kwame and the other two passengers by the port gunwales unsure of what they should now do.

The Dutch lady broke their silence and told Kwame he must be careful when Bidrock was around. She explained to him that she had had a long talk with Hicks about Bidrock. Hicks told her that Bidrock had been at sea since he was a boy. He had worked on slave ships and later on British war ships during the wars against Napoleon. He was a good sailor, knew the ways of the sea but was a bad man. He couldn't read or write and his head was full of terrible memories of the things that he had seen at sea. He knew no other life. He had no family that anyone knew of and certainly no friends. 'Be careful with him; there is no goodness in him and he'll never change. It's good that this is a well ordered ship because he's like an animal that has to be kept under control.'

The Dutch officer overheard this and said that it was a strange thing that Englishmen like Bidrock were also very proud of themselves. They didn't like foreigners. They felt superior to the whole world. Their leaders didn't like the slave trade and now used their navy to stop anyone else doing it, but they still despised and looked down on natives. 'They are not very nice people at all' said the officer.

Kwame was puzzled. White men had guns and ships. They were rich and could make many things that they brought to Elmina. They knew about God. There was so much to learn from them yet they had people like Bidrock and Croft, men who showed little respect to their superior officers. These people did not seem to like one another. How, he wondered, have they become so powerful?

Kwame left the deck to go to the foc'sle thinking that he'd talk to Hicks about this because all white men cannot be like Bidrock. Hicks wasn't like him. Were they from different tribes?

## CHAPTER FOUR

# BELOW DECK

The foc'sle was already lit by candles and their flickering light picked out the blue plumes of smoke from the sailors' pipes. The atmosphere was close and muggy. The cook – an older man called Jackson – had left a pot of boiled pork and beans and some ship's biscuits for their evening meal. Kwame sat down beside Hicks who was smiling and holding up a biscuit to the light that exposed two or three small holes in it. 'This little bugger has been half eaten before I picked it up' he said. On the bench beside him was a little splodge of blood, the remains of the beetles that had crawled out of the biscuit and which Hicks had crunched with his thumb. 'Never mind' he said, ' it'll still fill a hole in my belly'.

Bidrock and Croft sat silently on the other side of the ship eating their food, slurping and belching as if they'd never been fed. 'This stuff rots yer guts' Kwame heard Bidrock say to the other. Kwame smiled to himself. He felt the same about the food they were given. He ate it but at each meal he felt a terrible homesickness for his aunt's *fufu* and *Kenkey,* her boiled maize dough. He longed for a plate of *Kelewele,* the fried plantain with ginger and groundnuts his aunt gave him. He, too, was fed up with the boring food, the regular pots of salted beef or pork. When the cook gave them their tea each night, he would dream of the tamarind fruit juice he liked so much back home.

When he mentioned these things to Hicks, he was told that when they called in to Sierra Leone to top up on water, he might be able to buy some of his favourite food in the market beside the harbour. That cheered him up and put him in a calmer frame of mind to ask Hicks about Bidrock.

'Do you belong to the same tribe as Bidrock?' asked Kwame. Hicks thought this was a funny question. 'We ain't got no tribes in England' he said 'but then', he added, 'we're not the same, are we?' He went on: 'Bidrock's from London, poor bastard. He's had a hard life. I'm Cornish, from St Mawes near Falmouth. I speaks different to 'im and ye meet a better class o' person in Falmouth.'

'You play the fiddle' observed Kwame. 'Did your father teach you how to?' 'Nay, lad' said Hicks and then went on to tell Kwame about the most famous fiddler in Cornwall, 'a black man, just like you – black as the ace of spades he was but a great one with the fiddle.'

Hicks went on to explain that the black fiddler – Joseph Emidy – had once been a slave. His Portugese owner took him from Guinea to Brazil and then back to Portugal where he learned his music. The poor young man was caught again by and Englishman and brought to Cornwall. 'After that' said Hicks 'he never looked back. He played his fiddle. He made his own music. He married an English lass and he played all over Cornwall, in Falmouth and Truro. I see'd him in St Mawes and couldn't believe me ears. I saw 'im a few times and that made me want to play the fiddle. But it's harder than it looks and I'll never be as good as 'im'.

Kwame listened with wide eyes and a look of astonishment on his face. He had never imagined that someone taken as a slave could be like Joseph Emidy, a great musician, someone well known in a strange land.

Hick's could see the look of wonder and curiosity in the boy's face and said: 'Don't think other slaves were like 'im, lad. Talk to Jackson and Croft, even to Bidrock. Cap'n

Noble knows a thing or two as well. They'll tell yer about the slave ships they worked on but maybe you shouldn't hear about it. What 'appened to those poor buggers was awful. I'm glad the slave trade is no more; it was no work for Christian men.'

His work finished, Jackson sat down beside them. 'My poor old legs' he said. 'They need a rest. I'm getting to old for this life. What's you two natterin' about?' Hicks liked Jackson. He wasn't too fond of his cooking but thought Jackson was a good man and he liked to hear his stories from the past.

'We was talkin' 'bout slave ships' said Hicks. Jackson lifted his head and looked into the distance as if his mind was going back in time. He sat in silence for a few moments as if he was reliving part of his life and could not find the words he needed to talk about it.

'What I couldn't stand' said Jackson 'was the smell'. He said: 'You could smell a slave ship a mile off. Whatever we did, all that swabbin' and swillin' and cleanin' the boards with vinegar; but it wasn't enough. The stench of those poor souls living in their own shit below deck was ingrained in the wood. Even when we got back to Liverpool with a cargo of cotton, we could still smell it.'

'And the sharks' he said; 'They terrified me'. If one of the cargo died, we trussed 'im up and threw 'im overboard. As soon as he hit the sea the sharks were at 'im. See? They followed the ships. They knew they'd get a good feed.'

Kwame sat transfixed. His eyes were locked onto Jackson's face and so wide open it was as if he was reliving everything Jackson was talking about. In his mind's eye he could see it all and his head was full of questions.

'Did the slaves not fight back?' asked Kwame. 'Fante warriors would not let anyone treat them like that without a fight'. Jackson turned his head slowly towards Kwame and said 'We always worried about that, lad. Some did but only ever once. They were given a good lashin'. And some were lashed so hard they didn't survive. Funny thing was, you know, some of them wanted it to be like that. They'd rather be dead than captured. But a good lashin' kept the others quiet and we watched 'em like hawks.'

Kwame looked very thoughtful and said: 'I know why'. He explained: 'They say that when we die, we go home to our relatives and villages. They say that our ancestors are waiting for us so there is nothing to fear about death. Do you people not believe that?'

Jackson looked at Hicks as if to ask, how do you answer that? Hicks smiled and turned to Kwame and said: 'I don't know what to believe. Our preachers and God fearing folk say we go to heaven when we peg it. Mind you, they say that's true only for those who've been good and said their prayers an' that. Other poor buggers end up in Hell with the Devil. By their reckonin', most of us will end up there. And there'll be a special place in Hell for ships' captains, don't you think Jackson?'

'I've seen some brutal buggers in my time' said Jackson. 'Maybe they were the Devil! They were as bad to the crew as they were to the slaves. Them ships were prisons ruled by the gun and the lash.'

'Why did the sailors join such ships?' asked Kwame. 'Poor buggers had no choice!' said Jackson. 'They had no work. The captains got them drunk and lent them money and when they couldn't pay it back they forced them into jail. The only way some of 'em could get out of jail was to join the Guinea ship and go to Africa for slaves.'

'So they were just like slaves themselves?' said Kwame. 'Aye,' said Hicks. 'You're right there lad'. 'That's what 'appened to Bidrock and he was just a young'un at the time. He's had many a lashin' from a brutal captain. And he's lashed a few slaves in his time, too.'

'And that's why' said Jackson 'that Bidrock, just like his shipmate Croft, get drunk when they can. It helps them forget. They spend their money on drink and end up in jail so they have no choice but to get back on the Guinea ships.'

That night, Kwame could not get to sleep. He lay listening to the sounds of the ship and imagined that he was a slave trapped below deck, shackled to the floor with many others and not knowing what his fate would be.

He climbed into his hammock that night and tried to sleep holding tightly to his precious armband that helped him pray to his ancestors and to the sea spirits for their protection. He asked them to make sure he would be like Johan Neizer, the Fante merchant back home, and not suffer the fate of the poor souls that Jackson had talked about.

# Chapter Five

# Land Ahoy!

The weather was pleasant, with light breezes driving the ship forward on calm seas. Kwame liked it best in the mornings when the sun was bright and the water sparkled. But he liked the evenings as well when he could watch the great orb of the sun sink below the horizon casting the whole sky in a warm, deep, red glow that sharpened the shadows of the ship, its sails, ropes and masts. He liked the view from deck after dark, too. The sky was dense with bright stars. It felt to him that the whole world was at the centre of a vast sphere of a twinkling heaven.

He had lost count of the numbers of days they had been at sea. It seemed a long time and was surprised when the first mate, standing on deck with captain Noble and peering through his polished brass telescope shouted to all: 'Land Ahoy!' They had reached their first stopping place: Sierra Leone.

Kwame was excited by this news. He had heard of Sierra Leone as a place where freed slaves from America had returned to Africa to build a new country. He might meet some of them. *The Hope* needed fresh water and food supplies. The captain wanted to buy some new rope and to have some of the sails repaired. The sailors were keen on a shore trip and a break from the ship.

Kwame had overheard Bidrock and Croft talking together. They said they'd 'let their hair down' a bit on shore and nudged each other in mad encouragement as they spoke and laughed in anticipation of being back on land. Their laughter was coarse and their wide, open mouths showed off the gaps in their rotten and stained teeth. As they spoke loudly to each other, their frothy spittle dripped onto their greasy beards. Kwame looked on with as mixture of pity and horror and thought: 'These men are ugly'.

That evening the ship anchored off Freetown. After their meal, Jackson and Hicks sat together with their pipes and Kwame joined them, his head full of questions. The Dutch officer had told him that Sierra Leone was a troubled place. The freed slaves from America that the

British had brought in their ships back to Africa were not a happy group of people. They had suffered a lot from disease and the British did not treat them well. They complained a lot to the British Governor. There had been fighting with local chiefs and French ships had fired guns at their settlement during the war with Napoleon.

He told Kwame that despite all that they had built up a settlement, Freetown, and made sure they would keep their freedom. The harbour and river settlements were now very busy places. They grew crops. They had found that the land was good for growing coffee. The Dutch officer told Kwame that the freed slaves built a church and a school and once, when he was there on his last voyage, he saw the annual carnival that they organized with music and dancing in the streets.

Jackson confirmed what the Dutch officer told Kwame. He had been to the Sierra Leone river a few times and had seen the place grow and become very lively, with shops and traders and a busy trade on the river. 'But you have to be careful there' he said. 'There's too many temptations, particularly to get drunk!' 'And' he added, 'you've got to be careful how you speak to people. Them they call 'the Nova Scotians' speak English. They've got something precious that people up the river have never known: their freedom. The local chiefs don't like 'em cos they show them no respect. Woe betide anyone who treats them as if they was like everybody else.'

'Is it true' asked Hicks, 'that there's still a bit o' slavin' going on there?' Jackson told them that it was true. Some of the local kings up river – greedy, powerful people – still dealt in slaves, selling them illegally to American slavers who had managed to slip past the British navy vessels patrolling the coast. 'The Nova Scotians didn't like that' he said. 'They'd seen it all before and knew what would happen to those poor souls in the West Indies or in the southern states by the Mississippi.'

Kwame could barely contain his excitement and his eagerness to get ashore. He wanted to meet these freed slaves. Just as important to him, he wanted some proper African food and knew he'd be able to get it there. He'd give anything for some fried plantains and tamarind juice.

That evening, Captain Noble called them all together on deck and told them they would stay three days in Freetown. Everyone would get the chance to go ashore. 'But' he said, 'be warned. You'll be back at agreed times. You'll remember your duties on board and if you get into any trouble on shore, you'll suffer for it.' He looked sternly at Croft as if to say 'And you know what I mean by that!'

Bridrock and Croft looked at each other as if they were naughty boys with a secret understanding that they would ignore everything the captain had said.

The Dutch officer was keen to see Freetown again and show his lady around. He was keen to learn how much it had changed since his last visit. She was eager to see the school and the church that had been built, having heard that the freed slaves sang their hymns beautifully.

Hicks wanted to meet some of the Nova Scotians and talk to them. He hated the idea of slavery. At home, he had read pamphlets about it and thought it was wrong. He wanted to know what the freed slaves thought of life in Freetown.

Jackson wanted to buy in some fresh food supplies and make sure the water barrels were filled.

Captain Noble and Boydell wanted to meet the Governor and see if there were any chances of doing some business with local traders.

Kwame didn't know what he wanted to do on shore. He wanted to see everything, talk to everybody, eat as much as he could and see how the traders worked. For him, this was a visit to a new world and he couldn't wait to explore it.

# Chapter Six

# Sierra Leone

The trip to shore started badly for Kwame. He'd woken from sleep feeling excited about going ashore but was plunged into a deep gloom when he realised that he could not find his amulet. He kept it in his *kente* cloth bag and hung that on a nail beside his hammock. When he went to find it to help him with a prayer to his ancestors before leaving the ship to go to Freetown, it wasn't there. It was always there. He always checked it before sleep and last night it was there. What could have happened to it? He looked on the floor. He checked if it had fallen behind the ship's timber near his hammock but it was not to be found.

His mind was racing with questions and he felt both sad and angry. The amulet was his most precious object. It was his tie to the family back home. It was his link to his ancestors. Through the amulet he could talk to the spirits that looked after him. The sailors who had seen him with it called it his 'fetish' – a word that seemed to him to be rude and insulting as if the amulet was just a piece of trash – but to him it was the most precious thing imaginable.

Hicks came into the foc'sle and asked Kwame what he was doing. Kwame explained and Hicks helped him look around but to no avail. 'Reckon it's been filched' said Hicks. 'Who would do that?' asked Kwame. They looked at each other in silent agreement and with a nod of his head Hicks pointed to the hammocks of Croft and Bidrock. Both had gone ashore.

'One of 'em took it' said Hicks. 'They don't get their pay until we get to London and they'll need some money or something to barter with when they're ashore. You mark my words, they'll be after drink.'

Kwame was furious. He rushed back up on deck and could see that the shore boat Croft and Bidrock had taken for their trip had reached the landing stage at the river mouth. Fortunately he and the other two passengers were due to go next for their visit to the settlement. The boat was rowed by two African men – 'Nova Scotians' – who earned money ferrying sailors to and from their ships.

They spoke English and were surprised that Kwame could talk to them.

The Dutch officer and his lady sat quietly in the boat because they did not understand English very well. Kwame questioned the boatmen about what sailors normally did when they arrived on shore because he wanted to track down Croft and Bidrock as quickly as possible. The boatmen were very interested in Kwame. They were surprised he could speak English and Dutch. They were even more astonished that he was going to learn to be a trader in Holland so that he could return to the Gold Coast and make money. Their first thought had been that he was a slave but they were pleased that he was not. 'One day' they told him they hoped that 'there would be no more slavery and that all people, especially those still in slavery, would be free like them.'

Kwame heard what they said but he wasn't really listening. All he worried about was where he could find Croft and Bidrock. The boatmen were puzzled by him being so agitated but told him where he might find his shipmates.

Their advice was helpful. It took him no more than half an hour to find them and they were already sitting beside a wooden hut whose owner sold drink and tobacco. They should have been going to the fresh water man to order barrels of water for the *The Hope*. They had money from Captain Noble to pay for the water as well as for the boat to take it to the ship.

Kwame decided that he would move towards them as quietly as he could and then shock them by demanding that they return his amulet immediately. But he wasn't sure what he would do if they denied stealing it.

It was clear to him that Croft had already stolen a little of the ship's money to buy some palm wine and both had already drunk some of it and this made them feel happy and proud that they had managed to cheat Captain Noble to get a drink.

Kwame kept out of their sight and heard them talking.

'It's just wot we deserves' said Bidrock. 'A man has a right to a bit o' pleasure, don't he? If the greedy buggers paid us we wouldn't 'av to borrow their money, would we?'

'Wotch yer talking about? said Croft. 'Who's borrowin' money? This is our money! 'We're owed it!' Bidrock laughed at this. 'So we're not stealin' then?' he said and Croft replied: 'Nah. This is wages'. 'But we daren't take more of our wages' said Bidrock. 'Noble is a cunning and greedy old bugger wot counts every penny. He'll know if we nicked anything. How we goin' to get another drink?'

Croft tapped his nose with his forefinger and with a self-satisfied, evil grin and a wink of his left eye said; 'Don't you worry your pretty little 'ead about that. I've got a little something that'll get us some more drink, as much drink as we want.'

Unaware that Kwame was watching him, Croft put his hand in his pocket and pulled out the amulet. 'We'll get as much drink as we want with this little pretty' he said. 'Where'd you get that?' asked Bidrock. 'Nicked it from the blackie on board. He'll think he just lost it but we can turn this into good money and good money means drink! There's nothing else to do in this God-forsaken hole.'

As he said this, Kwame stepped in front of them and said: 'Give it back to me! You stole my amulet. Give it back!'

'Wotch yer goin' to do about it?' said Croft angrily. 'Steady on boy,' said Bidrock. 'We can talk about this'.

'There's nothing to talk about' said Kwame. 'You either give me back my amulet or you'll be in big trouble.'

'Get lost!' said Croft. 'If you don't want a good beatin', get yerself away from me!' 'Hold it!' said Bidrock. 'The lad's right. He's got summit on us. If he tells Noble about us, we's done for!'

Kwame said: 'Croft, the scars on your back from the lashing you had at Elmina haven't healed yet and you're asking for more! Are you mad? If I tell Boydell or Noble that you stole the ship's money for drink, you'll get such a lashing that you'll not survive it. Or worse, they'll leave you here. Give me back my amulet now and I'll not say anything to anybody.'

'Listen to 'im' said Bidrock. 'He's speakin' true. Give the lad 'is armband. We wants to get away from this hell hole and back 'ome.'

Reluctantly, Croft handed over the amulet to Kwame who was so pleased to get it back he stopped feeling angry. He almost felt sorry for Croft. But he did not show it. He looked him straight in the eye and said: 'Croft, you are a fool. You don't know what's good for you. But I'll not tell on you. Go and order the water barrels and then get back to the ship!'

The he turned to Bidrock and said: 'As for you, Bidrock, you should have more sense. You wouldn't survive the lashing you'd get from Boydell. Why would you risk your life for a drink of palm wine?'

Although he would never admit it openly, Bidrock knew that what Kwame said was true. He was angry with himself for being pulled along by Croft's mad scheme to steal money for drink and angry that an African boy had told him how stupid he was. He knew he had no choice but to do what the boy said. In his younger days, he would have given the boy a good beating for his impudence to teach him a lesson. Now, he realized, he wasn't as strong as he was so he had for once to do what was right for his own sake.

Kwame left both men and walked from the landing stage into the town, impressed by everything he could see: the buildings, the boats, the mouth of the river and lots of people, colourfully dressed and busy going about their work. It was a lively, noisy place. He could hear African drums from over the river. He could hear the sounds of the forest and that reminded him of home. He could hear singing coming from some of the chapel buildings. Most of all, he was impressed by the power of his ancestor spirits to lead him to recover his amulet. He said a silent prayer of gratitude to them as he walked along.

Near the big church, he met the Dutch officer and his lady. He did not tell them what had happened between him and Croft. He did say that he thought this was a wonderful place and that the people seemed very happy. The lady said that she thought the people were very proud; that they had worked hard to build their homes and to create their small farms out of what must have been a wilderness.

The Dutch officer said he didn't think Freetown would last long. The people did not like each other he said. Those who came from Nova Scotia were disliked by those who had always lived around the river mouth. They still bought and sold slaves and did not like the idea that slaves could one day be free. They did not like to see British troops around the place and resented the fact that these troops often stopped slave ships from leaving the coast for America and released their slaves to this land. The freed slaves worked hard and did not like the Sierra Leone people because they thought they were lazy and cheated people they traded with.

His lady said that the people from Nova Scotia were really clever and kind. They spoke English and African languages. They welcomed the slaves the navy had freed from the slave ships they had intercepted and they were building a pleasant town with many wood-framed buildings. The local people still built their houses in the traditional style with mud walls and thatched roofs. They had built chapels, a school, a hospital and the Hospitality Hall they had made was a wonderful meeting place for everyone. They worked hard and they loved God and sang beautiful hymns in church.

'Yes' said the Dutch officer 'that's all true, but they don't follow the church's rules on marriage and some of them still believe in witchcraft.'

Kwame listened intently to the two of them talking about the people in Sierra Leone. His mind was racing ahead thinking of the time he would come back to his land and become a successful trader like the people he could see here.

He walked back to the landing stage area with the Dutch couple to where there were warehouses. He turned a corner of the street and was suddenly confronted by men in a group arguing and shouting. Most were African, speaking English in an accent he had only recently heard. In the middle of the group, eyes flashing in anger and with their voices raised, were Croft and Bidrock. One tall, strong black man with greying hair and a powerful voice had his hands raised in a gesture of peace and was explaining something to the others.

'Please, brothers', he said. 'This is no way to go on. These men don't know our ways. They don't trust us. They don't understand us.' 'They said we were cheats!' exclaimed one man. 'They called us scheming bastards!' said another. 'We ain't heard language like that since Louisiana' said another. 'They said they'd get the soldiers to sort us out' said a young man. 'We told them, if they don't want to pay the price for the water, they could go without it!'

Kwame knew immediately what was wrong. In their stupidity and on account of all their bad manners, Croft and Bidrock had upset the water sellers. They couldn't agree on a price so the two sailors had become angry and abusive. Kwame decided to push into the group and to explain to the two of them that they had to agree the price and walk away. His plan was then to explain to the others that Croft and Bidrock were not really bad men, they were just ignorant and knew no better.

The tall man with the deep voice then spoke. 'Young man' he said, putting his hand on Kwame's shoulder 'you're a peace maker! The Lord will bless you. Where are you from? Are you a slave to someone from that ship?' Kwame was both pleased at the compliment but shocked at the question. 'No,' he said 'I'm not a slave! I'm going to be a student in Holland. I'm a Fante from Elmina'.

'God be with you', said the man 'but be careful. There are still people here who would clap you in irons and send you off on a slave ship. You are safe here in Freetown, but don't wander up river. King Jimmy's men are like snakes in the grass, still trying to make money from slaves.' The man went on: 'Be careful, too, with your shipmates. I've seen many white men like them in my time. They treat people like us badly. They think they're better than us. Some of 'em are decent souls but there's many 'o them are beyond redemption. The likes of those two are not welcome here.'

The Dutch officer and his lady stood in silence as they watched what was happening. After the water price was agreed and the group broke up, they spoke to Kwame. 'You're a brave young man' said the lady in Dutch. 'You'll go far in this life.' Kwame glowed with pride but he was still unsure about what he should say to Bidrock and Croft.

By the time he'd walked back to the landing area, the two of them were already there, arguing with one another. When Kwame came up to them they stopped and became silent but still with scowling faces.

Kwame was not put out by this; he knew now he could deal with Bidrock and Croft. For all their bad temper and surliness and threatening attitudes, men like them could be controlled. Kwame knew that now and he was not afraid. He could almost feel sorry for them for their lives were so brutal and hopeless but pity soon gave way to his dislike of both of them

CHAPTER SEVEN

# SAILING NORTH

From Freetown they sailed north into darker seas and cooler winds. Kwame felt the benefit of the warm, heavy clothes the Dutch officer had given him for journey. He felt secure in his friendship with Hicks and well looked after by the Dutchman and his lady. He felt confident that he could become like some of the men he'd met in Freetown and return home ready to impress his friends with his stories and his new skills and his plans to be a leader in Elmina.

The ship sailed well even as the swell on the sea became more menacing as the winds grew stronger. The air was fresh and clear but the crew made their evening amusements down below and not on deck. They smoked their pipes; they laughed coarsely at each other's tales of life at sea and of raucous nights in far flung ports. Hicks could sometimes be persuaded to play his fiddle but most of the time their lives on board followed the rhythms of the watch when work was followed by sleep and sleep by work.

Kwame kept himself busy helping out on deck and he took every opportunity to speak to his fellow travellers and the crew. As they neared the Canary islands, aiming to anchor at Santa Cruz for more supplies, Kwame had the chance to talk to Captain Noble and the First Mate, Boydell.

It was a fine morning. The ship was on a steady course and the sea had only a light swell. Noble and Boydell were in a relaxed mood confident that they were making good progress with everything under control. Kwame went up to them and caught their eyes as they were standing by the windlass near the prow of the ship.

'And what can we do for you, young fella?' asked Captain Noble. Kwame smiled, pleased that he had been given permission to speak and was not being sent away immediately. He had exchanged no more than a few words with either man throughout the journey but had heard a lot about both of them from Hicks.

'I was just thinking' said Kwame 'what is there in Santa Cruz, our next stop?' Boydell smiled at the Captain and said in a teasing way to Kwame: 'You'd better watch yerself there young man. Some o' them Spanish captains in the harbour there still steal people like you and take them to the sugar plantations in Cuba.' 'Don't take no notice of 'im' said Captain Noble. 'It's not like that anymore. There was a time when slave ships dropped anchor there and swapped their cargo – recaptured runaway slaves usually – and then sailed on to America but it doesn't 'appen no more, thank God.'

'But be careful' the captain said. 'The people there don't like us very much. They remember when we were at war. We remember that as well. The navy got its arse kicked there. Old Lord Nelson lost his arm trying to sink a Spanish fleet. They still celebrate that victory. Mind you, the poor buggers ain't got much to celebrate now. Nelson got his own back against Boney at Trafalgar though it didn't do 'im much good. He copped it there. A Frenchy rifleman got 'im. They brought his body back to England in a brandy barrel and made 'im a hero.'

'Whose 'Boney'?' asked Kwame and, his interest really aroused, now went on to ask: 'and what happened at Trafalgar?' Boydell answered: 'Napoleon, the Frenchman. We was at war with 'im at the time. Trouble-maker, he was; wanted to rule the world, he did.'

The captain turned away and walked back towards the stern of the boat and as he did so Boydell said to Kwame: 'He was there, you know'. He went on: 'He was in the navy as a boy. He's seen a lot; had a hard life. He fought in America. He's seen the slave ships. He's seen what they did to those poor souls on the plantations. He doesn't speak much about it. Some of us thinks he worked a couple of crossings with a slaver after he left the navy, but he won't say. But he was at Trafalgar.'

'But what happened? What is Trafalgar?' Kwame persisted although Boydell's attention was now turning to the ship and the sails and the direction of the wind. 'Trafalgar was a sea battle. Nelson was the Admiral of the Fleet and from his ship, *The Victory*, he fought the French fleet and destroyed it. That put an end to Boney and his plans. Well, it did for a while. Ask Hicks, he'll tell yer about it.'

Boydell then added: 'But don't pester the captain with your questions. He doesn't talk about these things anymore. He's a good sailor. He learned the hard way in the navy. He knows how to keep a tight ship and 'ow to handle rough sailors. Discipline's the thing. He's a stickler for discipline. Don't cross him or ye'll see what ye'll get: paying passenger or not, you'll get a good lashin!'

Kwame left Boydell and walked back along the deck to where the Dutch officer stood with his lady. There were so many questions buzzing in his head that he wanted to ask them that he couldn't decide where to start. He was thinking of Napoleon. He was thinking of people ruling the world. He was thinking of white men fighting battles at sea far from their homes. How did they know how to get to the places where they fought? The only battles he knew about were between the Fante and the Ashanti and they took place on land between different warrior armies. They were fought over land rights and slaves and in revenge for stealing. What does 'ruling the world' mean? Gods ruled the world, not people! Tribal leaders like the Ashanti King can rule in particular places; how can anybody rule the whole world?

He had questions about himself, too. Would he be safe in Santa Cruz? Could he really be captured as a slave? He remembered a conversation he'd had with Hicks about Joseph Emidy, the famous African fiddler that Hicks had seen play in Falmouth. Emidy had been a slave, owned by Portugese traders. They took him to Brazil and Lisbon in Portugal where he was able to earn a living as a violinist. The next part of the story that Hicks had told him worried Kwame because he knew it was possible that *The Hope* would call in a Lisbon on its way north to England.

Could he be taken into slavery like Emidy? Would anyone on board *The Hope* betray him to a slaver? Surely that was not possible now. Or was it?

Hicks had told him that Emidy was captured by an Englishman and put onto a naval vessel – the *Indefatigable* – which was being repaired in Lisbon during the wars with the French – as its ship's fiddler. He was kept on that ship for four years and must have been involved in battles with Napoleon's navy. They eventually set him free in Falmouth where he settled down and married and played the violin and composed music. Kwame had been puzzled at that. What did it mean to compose music? The songs and drumming that he knew hadn't been made up; they were just there. People knew them. Nobody made them up.

Kwame hoped to talk to the Dutch people but before he could do so they all heard shouts of 'Land Ahoy' and when they looked ahead to starboard they could see on the horizon the dark blue mountains of Tenerife. Santa Cruz was in sight and the sailors scurried around the ship to prepare for entering the harbour.

The Dutch major was always keen to watch how the men worked and to study how captain Noble managed them. He was impressed that Noble could keep such a sullen, scruffy and shifty pair like Bidrock and Croft under control and wondered why he even allowed scum like them on board. His lady used to tell him that there was goodness in everybody and that if these men were treated properly they would behave better, but the Dutchman just didn't believe it. 'When men have been turned into brutes' he said, 'it's not possible to turn them into men again'.

Kwame left them to go back to the bow of the boat to watch land approach and to wonder what he would see there.

## Chapter Eight

# Into the Bay of Biscay

The visit to Santa Cruz was uneventful. They got fresh water and fruit and salted beef and fish. Kwame's visit to shore was a short one. The town of Santa Cruz was nothing like he'd ever seen. Behind it were bare mountains. Where were the trees? he wondered. The building he learned was the church, was much bigger than the church he'd seen in Freetown. He had never before seen the inside of a building like this with its stone arches and walls of gold. There were large stone buildings with arched windows greater than anything he had ever seen. These white men were powerful, he thought.

Hicks explained that the Spaniards who owned it all were rich. 'They're arrogant, cruel buggers as well' he said. They got their money – gold mainly that they nicked from the locals – from South America and Cuba. They've done their share of slavin' as well. They've always been good sailors though, and we've had a few wars agin 'em.'

Kwame liked listening to Hicks explain things. It was like listening to a story teller. He told Kwame about how Spaniards tried to rule the world as well as the French. 'But they ain't like us English' he explained. 'They's catholic, see?' 'See what ?' asked Kwame, 'what's catholic?'

'They believe different things about God' said Hicks. 'You mean they've got a different God?' said Kwame. 'No' said Hicks. 'It's the same God, but they worship him different and their guy in charge – the Pope they calls him – lives in Rome and gives orders from there...in Latin – wot people can't understand. With us it's different. We speaks English and don't believe in Popes. The Dutch pair on board are like us. They don't speak English – not at 'ome anyway – but they aint catholics and they don't like Spaniards and have had a few wars against them too.'

Kwame was puzzled. The more he learned about these strange, white people the less he understood. They stayed two days in Santa Cruz and Kwame was pleased to leave. The next part of their journey could bring them near its end. Captain Noble let it be known that they might call in at Lisbon but if they had enough water they would press on to the English Channel.

Jackson, the cook, thought they'd not need to stop over in Lisbon, in Portugal. They'd got plenty of supplies in Santa Cruz and as the weather got colder, everything in the food barrels would stay fresh for longer. And people would drink less water, he said.

Jackson had taken a liking to young Kwame. He felt sorry for him, an African boy going to spend a year at least in Holland. Jackson didn't think much of Holland. It was a flat, damp country in a constant battle with the sea which threatened to overwhelm it. As far as he could tell, Dutchmen spent a lot of time building up great dykes to keep the sea out. But they were good sailors and good businessmen.

Jackson spoke to the Dutch officer to find out if Kwame was going to be looked after when he got to Holland. 'Of course!' said the captain. 'He'll be put in lodgings with a lady in Delft who runs a small school and whose husband is a trader.' He explained that Kwame could go to the school and also spend some time in the warehouse to learn about trade. There was enough money from Kwame's uncle to pay for it all as well as for the cost of his passage back home in a year's time. He also explained that although he would not be able to see Kwame much on account of military duties, his lady would make sure to check on him from time to time.

Jackson said he was pleased to hear that but wondered whether it was all true. He'd seen a lot in his time at sea. He'd seen all the ugly sides of slavery and his memories of what he had seen sometimes frightened him. He no longer trusted anyone; he'd seen how horrible people could be, even when they seemed to those around them to be upright, Christian men of business. He'd seen black people in England, some of them recently freed from their slavery, living like dogs around the docks, begging for food or for a berth on a ship. He'd seen some men among them rounded up and dragged back into slavery. He worried that Kwame might suffer a similar fate. The boy was clever, but he was going to be alone. He was obviously brave but he did not know the ways of the white man's world.

What reassured him a little about Kwame's safety was that the Dutch lady passenger seemed to like the boy. They spent time together, laughed a lot and were clearly interested in one another and were learning a great deal from one another. She was a good teacher. Would she be able to protect him from the trials he would face in Holland?

The journey north was pleasant. The skies were clear; the breeze was steady and *The Hope* rode the waves with very little rolling or pitching. There was time for everyone to look around. They saw gannets with their great wings diving for fish. They saw schools of dolphins and at night they saw the star-filled skies. On some nights, before they had entered European waters, Hicks entertained them on deck with his fiddle.

The Bay of Biscay lay ahead. Jackson explained to Kwame that he'd have to find his sea legs all over again when they got further north into the Bay. He'd been through many a storm in these waters and most sailors feared this part of the journey. Kwame smiled anxiously. He did not want to show he was frightened. In fact, he was quite excited at the prospect of seeing a storm at sea but he was a little worried. 'Keep yerself warm and dry' said Jackson 'and if you can, stay below deck; up here's no place for a young'un if a storm breaks in the Bay.'

Kwame told Hicks what Jackson had said but added, much to Hick's amusement, that he wouldn't be worried by a storm because he prayed to the sea God and gave his amulet a good rub so that he knew he would be safe.

'Kwame, boy' said Hicks, 'don't you believe it. Gods don't help us. Some people think that Gods don't even exist!'

Kwame looked at Hicks with an expression of disbelief and thought to himself: 'how can anyone say that?' 'They say', said Hicks, 'that men invented Gods to help them explain things they didn't understand.' He went on: 'But we've got reason and we can work things out. We don't need people mumbling prayers and sermons and tellin' tales from old books to show us how to live or what to believe.'

Kwame was worried now; he didn't think it was right or safe to criticise the sea God. 'The truth is' said Hicks 'we've got to get free of those old ideas; they are like chains holding us back. Those Frenchies had the right idea when the strung up the priests and burned the churches!'

The ship's bell rang and Hicks had to go up on deck for his shift. As he left Kwame, he patted him on the head and said; 'Don't worry lad, this ship's seen some rough seas and pulled through. Pray to your sea God if you want.' With a teasing laugh he said: 'It won't do any harm'.

Kwame followed Hicks on deck and although the sea was beginning to churn and the sky darkening and the wind was blowing, there was still time to watch a watery sunset. The Dutch people had the same idea so Kwame joined them and told them about what Jackson and Hicks had said. They told him they were not looking forward to crossing the Bay and wished they were on board a larger vessel.

'Do Dutch people laugh at their Gods and their wise men?' asked Kwame. The lady laughed at the question but knew the boy wanted a proper answer. 'No' she said. 'We are God-fearing people, not like some of the English or French people.'

Just as she said that, Croft and Bidrock came up to them and told them to get off the deck. 'There's work to do ere' they said 'to get the ship ready for the coming storm'. Bidrock said 'An we don't want no bloomin' landlubbers in our way'. Jackson saw this and said to the sailors 'Calm down you two' and then to the passengers he said 'Don't worry about them. They'll do their jobs well enough but don't expect good manners from them'

'What's wrong with them?' asked the Dutch lady. 'That's a question!' said Jackson. 'There's more like them back home – old sea dogs with all the goodness knocked out of them'. He went on: 'It's the war that did for them; both were forced as young 'uns into the navy and saw some terrible things. When the war finished they had no work; they got into trouble fighting and stealin' and fetched up on the Guinea ships drinking their wages.'

'You're not like them' said Kwame 'and you've been at sea all your life.' 'That's another story, lad' said Jackson. 'I know no other trade but I've kept sober. I've got a keen weather eye on the world. More than anything, I keep thinking about things. In port, I read the papers, talk to people, go to meetings. Since the war ended, things have changed and they've got to change more. People like us, ordinary folk, won't put up with things anymore.'

Jackson walked off leaving Kwame puzzled. What funny people these were, thought Kwame. They go to war. So do we Fante, but only when we are being attacked. Some of them don't respect the Gods. Jackson wants to change things, but doesn't he know that change is something the Gods decide – or sometimes the Chief – and that all we can do is pray that the Gods are on our side. With these thoughts running through his mind Kwame thought he'd ask Hicks what he thought of Jackson.

'Jackson?' said Hicks with a raised eyebrow, curious to know why Kwame wanted to know about him and then, after a few moment's thought, said: 'I like 'im. He's a good man. Didn't used to be; was just like most of 'em, brought up at sea and nearly ruined by drink. But then he met people a'shore who helped him see things different.'

'In what way?' asked Kwame, somewhat bemused by the idea that different white people looked on the world in different ways. As far as he was concerned, the world was as it was and would remain the same no matter how different people looked at it.

'Like me' said Hicks, 'he thinks things should change. It's not right that ordinary folk are poor and have to do as their so-called "betters" tell 'em. Farm labourers are treated as bad as animals. Bairns work in dangerous factories. Bosses don't treat 'em good.' Becoming angrier by the minute as he explained things to Kwame, he said; 'If the lairds of the land treated their labourers with as much care as they looked after their animals – their horses and dogs wot they go huntin' with – the people of my country would be a lot better than they are. Our country would be a lot better than it is! We've got to turn this world upside down and speak up for our rights!'

Kwame's mind was racing. He loved to hear Hicks talk though he did not really understand what his words meant but he felt himself agreeing with Hicks, sharing his feelings as he spoke.

'There's lots that thinks like this now' said Hicks 'but they gets into trouble for doing so – locked up in prisons or worse: hanged. Things 'ave to change and they will. We are the many; them that keeps us down are the few'.

'When will the change come?' asked Kwame.

'I don't know' said Hicks, 'but its coming and I hope it comes soon; people have suffered too long.'

By the time this conversation finished, the night had closed in. The wind had grown stronger and the ship was rolling and pitching as the sea became angrier and started to crash in great plumes of foam across the bow of the boat. The ship's bell rang to call up the sailors who had been resting and Boydell came from his cabin to urge the passengers to go below deck.

It was not comfortable there. The ship pitched and rolled violently. The wind howled and the boat sounded like a drum being beaten by a mighty hand. Kwame could hear voices through the noise, men shouting orders to haul in sails and batten hatches and to man the pumps. This was the Bay of Biscay at its worst.

He remained in the foc'sle as he had been ordered to do but being a brave and curious lad and trusting the sea God to look after them all, he was determined to go on deck and see what was happening.

Everyone was busy. No one had time to talk and the danger they were in was obvious. Great waves that seem to come from nowhere hung over the ship, blanking out the little of the dark sky they could see and threatening to overwhelm them. The sailors pulled on ropes; they worked the pumps, they tied everything that was loose on deck so that nothing rolled around.

This went on for several hours during which time Kwame watched and prayed and kept out of the sailors' way lest he interrupt their work. As dawn started to break, the sea became quieter; the wind dropped a little and on Boydell's advice, the men were stood down for rest. Only Bidrock remained on deck charged with holding the ship's steering wheel steady on the course that had been set.

Bidrock was in no fit state to do this work. Kwame saw that he was exhausted so he went up to him to ask if he needed help. At first, Bidrock was suspicious and looked angrily at the boy and was tempted to tell him to go away but Kwame ignored him and put his hand to the wheel to help him. Bidrock felt immediate relief. He had felt his strength leaving him and found the wheel difficult to keep steady but Kwame's hands and arms were strong and Bidrock knew immediately the value of the boy's help.

After about an hour, Bidrock was relieved and told to rest. Croft took over from him but he did not want Kwame's help and told him so. Bidrock and Kwame – both wet through to the skin and hungry – went below deck where the others were still sleeping in their hammocks. 'You're a good lad' said Bidrock to Kwame. 'I couldn't 'ave done me shift without you'. At that, he collapsed into his hammock and fell into a deep sleep.

Kwame looked at him and thought that this was an old man who should no longer be at sea. Back home, he'd be an elder, someone who was looked after in his hut and no longer required to fight or to work. Pleased that the sea God had protected them all, Kwame stroked his amulet, said a prayer of thanks and flopped into his hammock and slept like a baby with a smile on his face.

The next day, Bidrock told his mate, Croft, about the help he'd had from Kwame and how he thought the boy was a good lad, 'a young 'un with good morals who would one day be a credit to his people.' Croft just laughed at this and said: 'You can't trust no black devils. They got no morals. They's savages'.

Bidrock wasn't shocked at this. He knew what Croft was like but he was angry. 'You don't know what you're saying and you aren't in a position to judge anybody. That lad helped me. And he saved your bloody skin back in Freetown!' Croft wouldn't listen. All he really cared about was to get this journey over with, to get off the ship and get a drink and spend his wages having some fun in pubs around the docks in London before he found another berth.'

Bidrock was sorry for Croft and determined that he would have no more to do with him. They would part company in London and Croft could go to Hell as far as he was concerned. That's where he was going and no one could stop him, the bloody fool that he was.

When Kwame came on deck the next morning, Boydell explained to everyone that they had come through the worst of the storm and were now set fair to their next stop, the Scilly Isles. They would get fresh water there and then make the final run home to London.

Boydell was a happy man. He knew Captain Noble did not want to go back to sea after this trip and that he, Boydell, would probably be asked to be the captain. He'd learned the ropes and knew the sea and had had a good teacher in Captain Noble.

Hicks was pleased that the journey was coming to end, too. He didn't want to return to the sea. He wanted to stay in England, make a living playing his fiddle and working to spread the message that the world needed to change. He wanted to help ordinary people understand that their troubles, their poverty and their government could all be changed if they joined together to fight for their rights as free born Englishmen.

Jackson did not want to return to sea either. Like Hicks, he was going join with others to fight for change. His passion was to oppose the slave trade and abolish it forever. He'd seen the slave ships. He'd seen how slaves were worked and punished in the Americas. He'd seen that people from Africa were treated as if they were not human beings and he hated those who thought that it was their God-given right to own slaves. He knew people in London who shared the same views and he wanted to help them as much as he could.

The Dutch people were pleased with the news. They had feared further delays and the possibility of stopping in Lisbon and they really wanted to get back to Holland. The Dutch officer thought he might be sent on after a while to the Far East to the Dutch colonies there. His lady would stay with her family and continue her studies into the geography and customs of Africa. Her stay in the Gold Coast had strengthened her interest in Africa and its people and she wanted to make sure that Kwame would be well looked after in Delft. She, too, thought the world had to change and in her conversations with Jackson, she had come to understand that slavery was against all the principles of her Christian belief. When she got off this boat, she would explain this to people.

# Chapter Nine

# To Scilly

The journey north after Biscay was easy. The days were short and the nights especially were very cold. Kwame had never experienced cold like it and spent as much time as he could below decks. He amused himself talking to Hicks and Jackson, even to Bidrock who now often asked about Kwame's family back home and what his plans were for the future. He liked it when Hicks played the fiddle after his shift on deck and Kwame even learned the tunes and could hum them in his head. He played *Oware* with Hicks – always beating him – and even taught Bidrock how to play it.

He was excited by the prospect of the journey's end and the beginning of the next phase of his life in Holland and then his return home to Elmina to make his fortune.

Hicks told him that he was looking forward to a short stay on Scilly. 'It's a good place' said Hicks. 'The people there are friendly. They know a lot about ships and we can get a few repairs to the boat done there. We can get some good food, too! And maybe some good beer! They know how to look after jolly sailor boys like us!'

'Wot I likes best', said Hicks 'is to get a good wash and get some of me clothes washed proper. If we've time, I'll get some new soles on these sea boots. They've got a cobbler there who does a proper job!' He went on: 'I'll be smartened up for London and ye never knows, I might find myself a pretty lady who likes a sweet smellin' sea dog like me!'

They had two days sail ahead of them before the planned stop in the Scilly Isles. The weather had changed. The sea was calm. The wind was slight and *The Hope* was enveloped in fog. The sailing was easy but there was an air of anxiety among the sailors. Hicks explained to Kwame that Scilly was a beautiful place but was treacherous for ships. Ships had to find a route through the islands and from either side of that route there were jagged rocks on which many a ship had met its end. He told Kwame not to worry. Captain Noble had navigated these waters many times and if anyone could get them through safely it was him.

Nevertheless, Kwame held his amulet and prayed to the sea God.

As they sailed on, the weather did not improve. All on board were grateful that there were no high winds to deal with but the mist worried them. They were sailing as if blind and just had to hope that Captain Noble's maps and his knowledge of the sea told him where they were.

When Kwame woke up on the morning of January 19th, 1830, he was immediately aware of heated, anxious conversations among the crew. They were not sure that Noble had worked out their position properly. They could not see the islands on account of the mist that enveloped them like a blanket. The weather had turned for the worse. The sea had become rough and in addition to the mist there was rain.

Because of the bad weather, there were no pilot boats from Scilly likely to come and meet them and lead them in. 'That's bad' said Hicks to Kwame. 'Those lads row out in their gigs to ships like ours. They know the waters round these parts like the backs of their hands. But if they don't know we're 'ere, they can't come and fetch us!' 'But don't worry' he went on. 'Cap'n Noble knows wot he's doin'.

A newspaper, which appeared a month later, described the weather that day as 'unusually severe and boisterous'. Noble and Boydell were on deck and deep in conversation trying to work out what it was best to do.

Boydell thought they should drop anchor, wait out the bad weather and when it cleared they would see where they were. Noble disagreed. He would drop anchor but the sea was too deep so it would be pointless doing so. Their anchor chain just was not long enough to reach the bottom of the ocean. They agreed that they could not haul in the sails because if they did that, they'd lose control of the ship and could be driven onto the western rocks of Scilly.

Everyone on board was anxious and felt there was nothing they could do but wait and see if the weather would improve.

After what seemed an eternity of waiting, Captain Noble issued an order to Hicks who was at the wheel of the ship: 'Change course to starboard!' he shouted 'There's the Agnes light house!' Hicks heaved on the wheel and the others ran to ropes to change the angle of the sails.

Kwame looked hard through the gloom surrounding the ship to see what Captain Noble was pointing to but couldn't see anything. Boydell asked Noble: 'Are you sure?' because he couldn't see the St Agnes lighthouse either. 'As sure as any man can be' said Noble. 'We'll be at St Mary's soon enough'.

'How long is soon enough?' wondered Kwame. He leaned as far as he could over the gunwale to see if he could see better where they were but no lighthouse came into view. What he did notice was that the sea beside the ship had changed colour. It was no longer the dark grey of deep water but had a bluey green hue to it that Kwame knew was a sign that it was no longer so deep. He shouted to Boydell: 'Look! We're not in deep water anymore!'

Boydell knew immediately what that meant. If they had come past St Agnes's lighthouse, the water would still be deep. Because it was a lighter blue, he knew they had probably gone too far north. He told Noble this but the captain said all was well. They both stood staring hard through the mist and Noble shouted again: 'There! See! There's the Agnes lighthouse'. Boydell agreed. Through the mist and the fading light he, too, caught a glimpse of a white lighthouse. He realized, however, that they had instructed the helmsman to turn to starboard too soon and turned to give him a new instruction to turn a little to port because they were too close to the St Agnes shore.

Captain Noble nodded his agreement with this but added that, now that they knew where they were, they should drop anchor and wait the for the miserable weather to clear. The order was given: haul in the sails and prepare to drop anchor! The men scurried around deck to do what was needed. Kwame and the Dutch couple watched what was happening and felt a strong feeling of relief that they would soon be on land. In no time at all, they heard the clinking of the anchor chain against the capstan as the anchor dropped into the water. In a moment, the anchor chain was fully extended, the forward movement of the ship was halted. The sails were quiet and all seemed still.

Then it happened. There was a loud scrunching thud followed by a squealing and tearing roar of wood being ripped from the ship. The whole frame of the boat shuddered and the sea gushing into the hull drowned the alarmed shouting of the people on board. The ship keeled slowly over to starboard and settled, broken on the rocks they had neither anticipated nor seen.

The shock of collision had sent the crew and everyone on board flying across the deck and when they picked themselves up, shocked, hurt, and crying for help, there was an air of panic and of fear. Where were they? Would the ship slip off the rock? How could they save themselves?

Captain Noble pulled himself up and issued an order: 'Abandon ship! Cut the boats free! Save yourselves!' Hicks and Jackson and the Dutch major leapt into action and untied the rowing boats from their stations and started to lower them into the sea. The others gather around ready to climb into them. Noble pointed in the direction of the land he'd seen and said: 'Row in that direction!' He watched till everyone was on board the boats, took a last look at his stricken ship and climbed into his boat releasing the rope that had tethered it to *The Hope.*

Within a few strokes of the oars, both boats pulled away from the wreck. The people in them were shocked, wet and cold but hopeful that they would soon reach land. Kwame gripped his amulet and said a silent prayer of thanks to the sea God. He looked around and saw that his fellow passengers were safe and that Hicks was in control of the oars. Bidrock was lying on the floor of the boat groaning in pain. Noble and the others were not far from them, all safe in their boat.

At that moment, Kwame allowed himself an inward smile. He was no longer frightened. The wreck of the boat was terrible but they would survive it. His Gods were with him.

Captain Noble explained later to the islanders who rescued them and cared for them that what happened next was a tragedy. As Noble's boat pulled away from *The Hope*, the main mast of the ship snapped at its base and came crashing down onto the other boat. The people in it had no chance. Their boat was cut in half. They were flung into the dark, cold water and disappeared in an instant into the churning sea. They tried to find them but could not do so and after half an hour or so, gave up searching and struggled to reach the shore.

The four who survived – Noble, Boydell, Jackson and Croft – reached the shore of what they thought at first was St. Agnes but Noble realized that this was not the case. A wide beach like the one they had reached did not exist on St Agnes. They grounded their boat and sought shelter, huddled together for warmth under a grassy bank at the edge of the beach.

They sat there and waited. It was not long before some islanders came to the beach having heard of the wreck and took the crew back to their homes in Higher Town, the main village of the island.

CHAPTER TEN

# THE AFTERMATH

The people of St.Martin's – about two hundred in all – were poor. They led hard lives working the land, looking after animals and fishing. Sometimes, not as often they hoped, they could take their gig out to a waiting ship to help it navigate the rocks around the islands. They were paid for this but it did not happen often to them; the St Mary's people hogged that trade. Some of them, the skilful sailors among them had often rescued people from ships wrecked on the dangerous rocks of Scilly. Nearly all of them, especially the young ones collected 'wreckage' that was washed up on the shore from ships that had been lost at sea. For some, a wreck was a cause of some joy; they'd get something for themselves from it.

On the morning of January 20th 1830, the young men of the island came to Great Bay to see the wreck of *The Hope* and offer any help they could. As soon as they stepped onto the beach from the path that led to it, they came across the huddled sailors and saw the wreck of the ship lying at an angle in the sea with waves breaking gently across its deck

They knew what to do. Some among them led the men to Higher Town to help them into dry, warm clothes and to feed them. Others began the work of inspecting the boat. They rowed boats around the island to the wreck and checked it for signs of life but found none.

Later in the day, they found three bodies washed up on the beach near Little Bay: those of two men and a young, black boy.

During the following days, the islanders heard the story of *The Hope* and became aware that one passenger, the Dutch officer's lady, was missing and despite their careful search of the rocks and the coast around the island, she was never found.

The islanders sent messages by boat to St. Mary's to tell people there about the wreck knowing that they would send letters by the next ship travelling to the mainland that could be passed on to the ship's owners in London.

During this time, the islanders arranged with the vicar of the church to bury the three travellers from Africa and to help the survivors of the wreck to return home.

They gave each a Christian burial although they did not know whether the black boy – the African boy – was a Christian or not. The vicar said it did not matter. In the eyes of God he was a human being made in his image and would find his place in heaven.

Over the next few weeks, at the request of the owners of the ship, islanders took from the ship most of its cargo. There were 175 casks of palm oil, 450 elephants' tusks, 7 boxes of gold dust, 1000 silver dollars and some boxes of pepper. The cargo was eventually shipped to London.

Over the next few months, as *The Hope* was smashed up by the sea, islanders collected wood from it for their fires, ropes for their own use, pots and pans, knives and forks, oil lamps, canvass from unused sails, maps and charts from the captain's cabin, a sextant, compasses and much else. By the summer of that year, there was nothing left of *The Hope*.

Captain Noble retired to his home in Bristol. Boydell returned to the sea but not as a captain. He had a reputation to build for no ship owner would trust a man who had wrecked a ship. Jackson retired from sea to work as a cook at an inn and to spend time with his political friends campaigning for people to be allowed to vote for their members of Parliament. Croft found other 'Guinea' ships to work on for men like him knew of no other life. In time, the families of the Dutch major and his lady and of Hicks the fiddler learned about the wreck. In Bidrock's case, there was no family to be told of his fate.

Months later, Kwame's family received news of his death by letter from Holland. It was delivered by a Dutch naval vessel that had been sent to the Gold Coast to recruit Africans to become soldiers and sailors who would be sent to the East Indies to protect a Dutch colony there

# AFTERWORD

All stories have a history. This story began, at least for my granddaughter who first noticed the African boy plaque, in St Martin's churchyard, with questions I could not answer. Who was this African boy? Who placed the plaque in the churchyard? Why? Was the boy a slave? Did anyone ever find out if his people in Africa ever learned what happened to him?

There can be no happy ending to the boy's story. But we now know about the plaque and the African boy has left us with a treasure of questions to think about. His life, whatever it was in reality, has not been forgotten.

We cannot now know the real truth about this boy buried on St Martin's. We have since learned about *The Hope*. Nigel Pocock, an historian and regular visitor to Scilly, was the person who, as a result of his researches into the history of slavery and into shipwrecks on the islands, decided to place a plaque in the graveyard to remember the lad. He got permission to do so from the then vicar of Scilly, Father Guy Scott. That was in 2010. Guy Scott willingly gave his permission for a plaque because it was a small contribution to the memory of the anti-slavery movement that 200 years before had persuaded parliament to make slave trading illegal.

Nigel commissioned the plaque from a monumental mason in London and together with Father Guy agreed on the biblical quotation written on it. Like us, Nigel does not know for sure anything about the African boy. He thinks that he was probably about six years old, sold as a slave, and was likely being taken unwillingly to Europe as a kind of house pet for some rich man to show off to his friends. That sort of thing did happen in those days. It is said that some African children taken in this way were kept until they were young men and women and then pushed out into the world to look after themselves. The African boy on St Martin's did not suffer that fate.

On May 16th, 2010, they placed the plaque in the graveyard and held a church service when they sang some hymns, written by Charles Wesley and Isaac Watts. Members of the St Martin's congregation were there as well as some visitors to the island including a Ghanaian

friend of the Pocock family. She is not related to the
African boy but her presence emphasised the boy's origins
and his belonging to a place with its own unique history
and memories. The service is remembered as being a very
simple one but very moving and to all who were there a
very special occasion.

People who notice the plaque may wonder about what
brought the African boy to Scilly. No one can really
know. The people who placed the plaque were thinking
about the boy in the light of the horror of slavery. By
remembering the boy they were saying on our behalf that
they were sorry for what he and his people suffered.

They were saying, too, that we all should remember him
and people like him for we have all benefitted from their
suffering. The slave trade brought riches to this country
that were made possible by the suffering of captured slaves
shipped from Africa to the Americas. In England, great
country houses were built and furnished with the profits
earned selling slaves. Cities like Bristol and Liverpool
flourished with the money their merchants made from the
slave trade.

It was a business from which many profited: the ship
builders, the merchants, the manufacturers who made the
beads, weapons, pots and pans, arm bands and cloth that

were traded for captured human beings who were sold to plantation owners growing cotton and sugar in America and the Caribbean.

Was the African boy a slave? We do not know. He might have been. On the other hand, he could have been as the story here describes him: a young, ambitious African going off to Europe to learn how to be a trader. Members of the crew of *The Hope* could have once worked on slave ships or on the ships of Nelson's navy during the French wars. They could certainly have been cruel, brutal men for the lives of ordinary seamen those days were hard and dangerous.

We will never know the real story of the African boy but we can continue to imagine it. With our stories about boys like him we can get close to the real truth about them. And we can be inspired to find out more about other Africans and the countries they came from and about what we did to them and how their stories became part of our stories. Their lives are part of our lives; their history is one that we share.

This particular African has not been forgotten. His memory evokes sympathy in all those who read the plaque dedicated to him. For those with a Christian outlook, the inscription on the plaque – 'I shall set your captives free' – is consoling.

A few words that are better known are the ones I shall encourage my grandchildren to think about. Josiah Wedgwood, the potter, made a famous anti-slavery plate in 1787, nearly half a century before the African boy lost his life. That plate, sold in thousands, helped spread the message that slavery should be abolished. His image of the kneeling, chained African was surrounded by the words:

'Am I not a man and a brother?'

These words inspired the anti-slavery movement at the end of the eighteenth and beginning of the nineteenth century. Sadly, time has not diminished the need to answer the question they pose.

Lightning Source UK Ltd.
Milton Keynes UK
UKOW04f0615281217
314965UK00001B/64/P